ClaRa's CRazy CURls

by
Helen Poole

Little Clara Day
was very, very small.

But what was **most** extraordinary was her hair was really **tall**!

She didn't need a pencil case,
a schoolbag, or lunch box,
instead she stored her gear...

in her **big, STRONG** curly **locks!**

But Clara often **wished**
that her hair could reach the skies.
The tallest hair in all the world!
And maybe win a **prize!**

One night in the bathroom,
Clara spied a jar up high.
The label read:

"Big and Beautiful Hair —
Guaranteed in just one try!"

Clara reached and grabbed the jar, without a second thought.

Big & Beautiful Hair

But she didn't use a little dab, instead she used A LOT!

Big & Beautiful Hair

That night while she was tucked in bed,
Clara never knew,

that while she lay there sleeping,
her hair **grew...**

and **grew...**

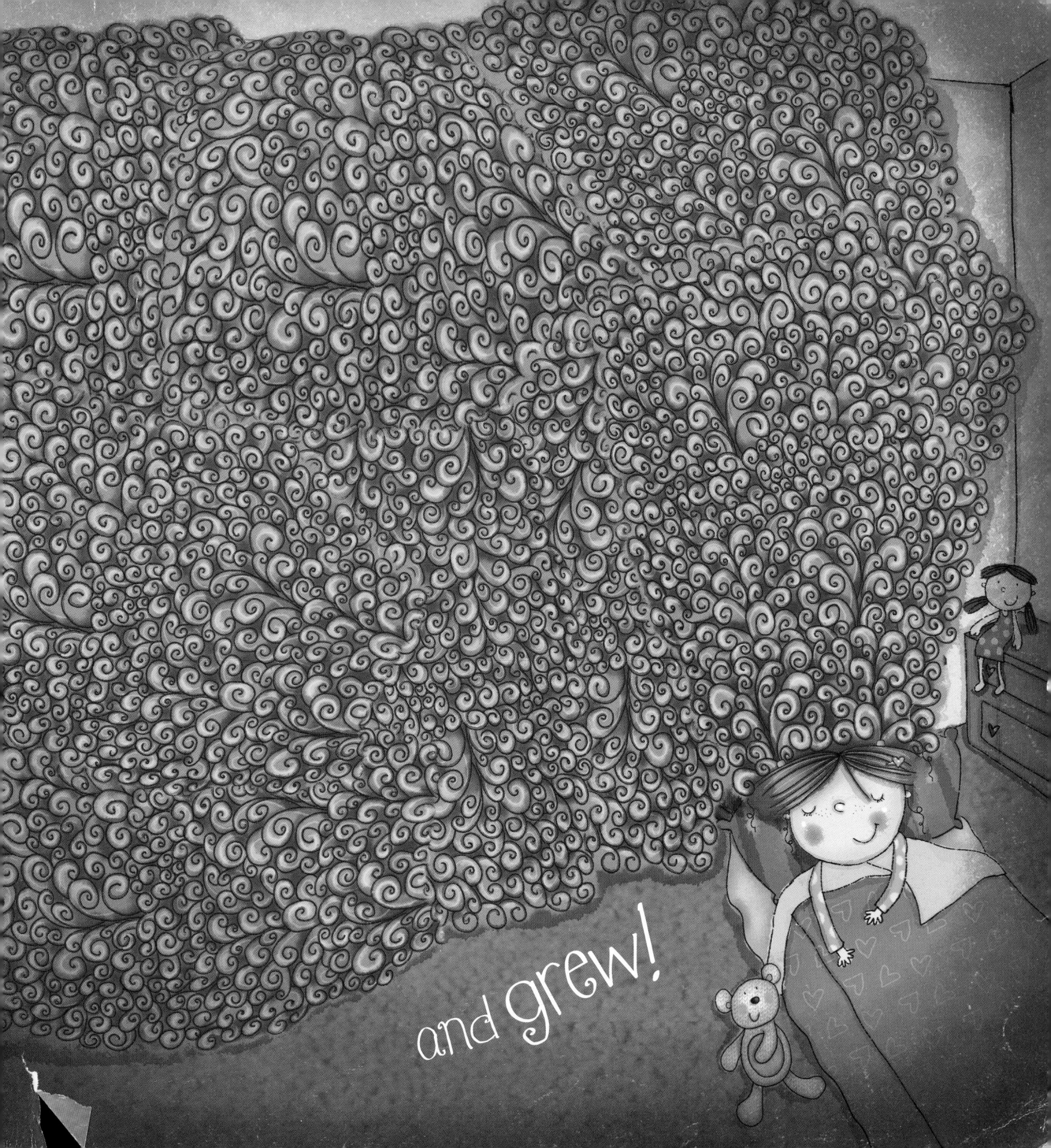

and grew!

When Clara woke next morning,
she was on the bottom stair.
She'd been slowly and quietly
pushed out of bed,
by her **crazy curly** hair!

"Yippee!" she yelled.
"It worked! HOORAY!"

Outside the birds all **snuggled** in their brand new **curly** nest.

Clara smiled and beamed with pride,

her curls were now the best!

Her hair was extra useful now,
she rescued cats from trees.
She cleaned out gutters on each house,

her neighbours were quite pleased.

And way up high in outer space
aliens clapped and cheered.

A planet made of **tickly curls** had suddenly appeared!

Back on Earth came crowds and crowds,
they couldn't help but **stare.**

Clara was now famous, people **loved** her crazy hair!

We ♥ Clara!

Clara here TODAY!

World's Tallest Hair!

But in between, among the clouds, that's where trouble **struck.**

Aeroplanes couldn't cross the curls.

Hot-air balloons got stuck!

The problems grew at Clara's school,
her friends couldn't see at all.
Unless she sat at the very back
alone against the wall.

Even worse was a trip to the cinema,
where her curls filled up the room.
Her friends couldn't see the film,
and Clara was filled with gloom.

Clara walked home all **flustered**,
she felt like a terrible friend.
She wished her hair was no longer so tall,
she wanted the **fuss** to end!

"Mum, I'm sorry. I lied to you!
I used all your fancy hair cream!
I only wanted my curls to grow.
That was my curly hair dream!"

"I'm glad you told the truth," said Mum
and she quickly grabbed the phone.
"Don't worry, my dear, this is easily fixed.
I'm calling Mrs Malone!"

Mrs Malone and her hair-cutting team went to work on that crazy hair.

They snipped and they clipped and they chopped and they lopped.

and it floated off into the air.

Clara realized that having **tall** hair – the tallest hair in the world –

wasn't as great as she'd **dreamed** it would be.
She was **happy** with shorter curls.

Her hair was still **taller** than average,
she didn't feel **gloomy** or **grim**.

She still used it to store all her school things

and went every week for a trim.

And often at night Clara wondered,
what happened to all of that hair?
Was it out there up high, coiling and curling,

still floating in the air?

Raintree is an imprint of Capstone Global Library Limited, a company incorporated
in England and Wales having its registered office at 7 Pilgrim Street, London,
EC4V 6LB - Registered company number: 6695582

To contact Raintree:
Phone: 0845 6044371
Fax: + 44 (0) 1865 312263
Email: myorders@raintreepublishers.co.uk
Outside the UK please telephone +44 1865 312262

ISBN 978 1 406 27569 8 (paperback)
17 16 15 14 13
10 9 8 7 6 5 4 3 2 1

British Library Cataloguing in Publication Data
A full catalogue record for this book is available from
the British Library.

Printed in China by Nordica.
1013/CA21301926

For all my wonderful family
with lots of love xxx